MW01147464

The Courage of Violet Hue

Jacqueline Mahan

authorHOUSE™

1663 LIBERTY DRIVE, SUITE 200
BLOOMINGTON, INDIANA 47403
(800) 839-8640
WWW.AUTHORHOUSE.COM

First published by AuthorHouse 2/15/2006

ISBN: 1-4259-0114-X (sc)

Library of Congress Control Number: 2005909976

Printed in the United States of America
Bloomington, Indiana

This book is printed on acid-free paper.

Cover illustration:Jacqueline Mahan

Dedication

It is with so much love that this book is dedicated first to my mother, Sandra, who really believed in my artistic gifts before I did. She steered me down that road, and so began my path in life.

As always, to my kookie family, Dad, Trish, Pat, Tugger, Pita and Biggie, I love you all! A special hug goes to Sophie Grandma for *all* the support. Thank you for always wanting the best for me. Ever upward! God bless you Granny, I love and miss you.

Finally, this lovely story is dedicated to every child who ever had or has yet to face an insecure moment. Remember: only YOU can decide what is true for you. No one else can, so don't let unkind words stop you from being your best. Rise above it and believe in yourself!

Chapter 1

"Give that back to me, Charlotte!" screamed Violet.

"Come and get it!" Charlotte yelled. She had that annoying smile on her face. She thought this was funny.

Charlotte ran ahead of Violet, waving the flower Violet had just picked for herself.

"What do you want with a stupid flower, anyway?" chided Charlotte.

"None of your business," said Violet. "Just give it back." Violet walked faster to catch up with Charlotte, but Charlotte skipped further ahead, singing, "Violet's stupid flower, Violet's stupid flower. I-I ha-have Violet's stupid flower!"

"Never mind," said Violet suddenly. "You can keep it." She slowed down, searching the grass for another flower.

Charlotte stopped. "Here! Take your stupid flower!" She threw the flower, but its lack of weight combined with Charlotte's conviction made the gesture look silly and overdone.

Violet kept her eyes to the ground, but she was aware of Charlotte's growing irritation. She continued to ignore Charlotte, searching for a new flower.

"You better not bring that stupid flower to school tomorrow!" called Charlotte.

"I'll bring it if I want," said Violet.

"Fine, 'Flower Baby,'" said Charlotte. "Violet Flower Baby!" Charlotte sang. She laughed at her own joke, and danced down the path toward her house.

Violet walked over, picked up the partially crushed flower lying on the dirt, and gently smoothed its crumpled petal. She looked after Charlotte, who was getting smaller with every step, then cut across Miller's field to her own back yard.

Pencils and crayons, markers and pens, are strewn on her bedroom floor. Violet sat with her back against her bed, sketchpad on her knees, pencil in hand. She looked at the flower, studied the colors, the shape of the petals and leaves. One petal was missing, another bent like an accordion.

This afternoon, as others, Violet spent her time before dinner alone in her room.

Violet's parents sat downstairs in the kitchen, at the table. Mrs. Hue worked on a crossword puzzle, while Mr. Hue read the paper.

"Where is Violet?" her father asks.

"Upstairs in her room", answers Mrs. Hue. "She's sketching."

"Why doesn't she sketch down here?" asks Mr. Hue.

"She is probably more comfortable in her own space. Let her be. She's happy drawing."

"It's not good for her to stay up in her room all the time."

"Oh, honestly, Dear!" said Mrs. Hue. "Violet's fine. She'll be down for dinner shortly and then you can ask her all about her day. Ask her about what she's drawing. Let her talk about it. You'll see how excited she is."

"Alright. Is her homework finished?"

"Why don't you ask Violet when she comes downstairs?" said Mrs. Hue, her eyes still on her crossword puzzle. She knew Violet had done her homework. Homework first, then free time. That was the agreement. Mrs. Hue knew her daughter was responsible enough to remember this. Mrs. Hue also knew Violet was very protective and private about what she drew and didn't like to share her "works in progress" with anyone, not even her parents.

Despite a little self-consciousness, Violet pursued her art. Her father was not against such a passion; he simply could not understand Violet's need for privacy. She was only ten. He thought if she could draw up inside her room, then she should be able to draw down in the kitchen, or the living room; places where the whole family gathered. Still, Violet did not feel comfortable with this. She refused to work anywhere but in her room when she was at home, showing her drawings proudly, *only* when they were finished.

It was at this time Violet bounded down the stairs, sketchbook in hand, to see if dinner was ready.

"Hi Mom, hi Dad. Want to see what I drew?" Violet asked.

"Sure, Honey," said Mrs. Hue.

"Yes!" exclaimed her father, "bring that book over here and let me see what my artist is working on."

"It's finished," said Violet. "I like it. See? It's a wildflower. I picked it on my way home." She held up the flower and the sketchpad simultaneously.

"What happened to the flower?" asked her mother.

"Oh," Violet hesitated, "it got a little crushed," she said. "But it's still good to draw from," she offered quickly. Violet directed them back to the drawing. "So what do you think?"

Mr. Hue held the sketchpad at arms length, examining the drawing, stealing a glance at his daughter. She certainly seemed proud of herself.

"Violet," her father started, why don't you ever paint or draw down here with us? We'd sure like to watch you."

Mrs. Hue looked at her husband, then at Violet who'd grown quiet, and cast her eyes to the floor. "Daddy, I don't like to draw anyplace else. It doesn't feel good to draw in front of other people," she said quietly.

"But you draw in school in front of your teacher and the other kids."

"They're all doing the same thing, though."

"Violet, I don't understand…" her father began, but Mrs. Hue interrupted him, saying, "Violet, Honey, why don't you go wash your hands for dinner, it will be ready shortly."

"Okay, Mom," said Violet, grateful for the opportunity to leave the kitchen.

After dinner that night, Violet thought about her father's words. Why *was* it so hard for her to do her artwork around other people? It was simply her own way of doing things, she guessed. Still, she wondered…

Maybe her father had a point. Violet thought about it a long while. *Okay*, she decided. She would take her sketchpad to school tomorrow. Maybe. Yes. Should she? Okay. Yes, why not? She would sketch during recess while the other kids played.

Chapter 2

When the bell rang, students scuffled around for their lunches and coats. Violet retrieved her sketchpad from her book bag, along with a few pencils and erasers.

At the lunch table, Violet and her best friend Amber sat together.

"I brought my sketch pad today," said Violet, biting into her sandwich.

"You did? Really? What are you going to draw?" Amber was aware of Violet's feelings toward her art. She knew Violet liked her privacy and was surprised at her friend's decision.

"Don't know yet." She looked thoughtful as she sipped from her juice box. Violet had no idea what she would draw once she got outside. She only hoped no one would bother her.

After lunch, the fifth graders went outside for recess. Children were playing tag and wall ball, jumping rope and swinging on the swings. Violet chose a shady spot under the big oak tree near the jungle gym and monkey bars. She sat on the bench and opened up her sketchpad. She looked around, wondering what to draw. The only thing she could draw was a blank. Mrs. White, her art teacher, always said, "If you can't think of anything to draw, draw anything." Violet watched the other children playing. Could she try to draw them? She looked at the big tree in front of her. Perhaps it would be better to draw something that didn't move. She could observe it more closely. With her pencil, eraser and sharpener by her side, Violet studied the tree. Then she began to draw, starting with the trunk and breaking the image out into branches, adding leaves. Violet held the pencil on a slant, using the side of the point for shading the tree.

As she worked, a small crowd gathered around her. She became aware of them watching her. She felt some strange tingly sensations in her stomach. She realized it was a mixture of pride, confidence and… something else. Violet swallowed. She continued to draw despite the growing commotion around her.

"Wow! Violet, you're good!" one boy exclaimed. Several other children nodded their heads in agreement. Violet beamed! This wasn't so bad. The children continued to watch, impressed with her talent. She relaxed a little. Violet was concentrating on the tree, and secretly enjoying the admiration of her peers.

Charlotte Brandt joined the crowd. She watched Violet draw. She looked at the tree, looked at the drawing, then at the tree again. Charlotte pulled a sour face. With a smirk and a dismissive wave of her hand, Charlotte said, "You can't draw!"

"You be quiet, Charlotte Brandt!" shouted Amber.

"Make me!"

"I don't make trash, I throw it away!"

"Yeah?" Charlotte stammered, "Well, I don't…I… you know what?"

SMACK!!!!

Violet's pad and pencils clattered to the ground.

"Charlotte, you get out of here, now!"

Charlotte laughed out loud and pointed, then turned and ran back to play with a group of girls at the other end of the playground.

Violet's smile faded. She cast her eyes to the ground. She bent to pick up her pad and pencils without a word. Everyone waited for Violet's reaction. She kept her cool in front of them, though her spirits had plummeted. Violet wondered now if the feeling in her stomach was closer to the truth: that she was better off just drawing in her room where no one could see. Perhaps she really wasn't that good at art. It was just something she liked to do, and she was better off keeping it to herself.

Violet fought back the tears in her eyes and the huge lump in her throat. Some kids had walked away, some lingered near, trying to console her and saying what a pain Charlotte could be. The bell had rung and the crowd on the playground had dispersed, children running and pushing to be first on line. How silly they all were. Rushing to be first to get back *into* school.

"Stupid Charlotte," said Amber. "Why does she always say those mean things? Don't listen to her Violet."

With her shoulders slumped and her head down Violet walked slowly, hugging her sketchpad to her chest. The day dragged on. Charlotte's words repeated in her mind: YOU CAN'T DRAW! YOU CAN'T DRAW!" She was a *brat*, Violet thought. Charlotte "Brat"! It was the only time she smiled all afternoon.

After school, Violet went straight home, ran up the stairs and threw her sketchpad to the floor. She would *never* bring it to school again. She would never draw in front of anyone ever, ever again!

Chapter 3

Violet was discouraged. She'd tried something different and it backfired. Charlotte "Brat" had come along and... Oh, she should have known better than to bring her sketchpad to school! She wouldn't even bring it down to her own living room! What was she thinking?

A loud knock on her door startled Violet from her thoughts. "Are you alright in there, Dear?" asked Mrs. Hue.

Violet pulled her arm across her teary red eyes and got up to open the door. Her mother walked in and sat on the bed. She listened sympathetically while Violet spoke about everything that happened at recess.

Mrs. Hue pulled her daughter close and hugged her tightly.

"You must feel terrible," said Mrs. Hue. Tears welled up again in Violet's eyes and she buried her face in her mother's neck, sobbing silently. Her mother smelled like lavender, which Violet found very reassuring. "I tried to draw a good picture. I even thought it was good 'til dumb old Charlotte "Brat" came over and ruined everything," she said, sniffing.

Mrs. Hue looked confused. "I thought her last name was Brandt," she said.

"It is," said Violet. "I just call her that cause that's what she is." Violet drew her shirt sleeve across her nose and sniffed.

"Now, Violet," her mother began, "is that necessary?" Mrs. Hue tried to conceal a smile. Her daughter could certainly be indignant at times.

"Violet, listen. There's no need for name calling, and your feelings may be hurt, but you did a very courageous thing today."

Violet looked at her mother, puzzled.

"You took a risk."

"A risk?"

"Yes. For you to take your sketchbook to school was brave choice."

"It was?" asked Violet.

"Of course. Where do you do most of your drawing?"

"In my room."

"Exactly. You won't even draw in the family room with Daddy and me, but you took your book to school and drew in front of the other kids. I'd call that brave. I'm proud of you."

Proud? Violet wondered how her mother did it. She could take a terrible, yucky experience and turn it into something positive. She knew some teachers at school who could do this, too. It must be a grown up thing, some magical power that only a few special adults have.

She opened her mouth to tell her mother about the flower-crushing incident, and then closed it. No big deal now.

"You took a risk, Violet. You did something outside yourself, something you wouldn't normally do. You did it even though you were afraid at first. You see?"

"But she said I couldn't draw!" Violet exclaimed. "She said it in front of everyone! Then she knocked my pad out of my hands. It got all dirty. I was…" she paused, "I was embarrassed." Her face scrunched up and a tear escaped from her eye and ran down her cheek.

Mrs. Hue looked at her daughter knowingly. "I'm sorry Honey. Really. It's no fun to be embarrassed in front of other people."

"Then she ran away laughing." Violet hung her head, looked at the floor. "Now they all think I can't draw."

"Well, I doubt that," said Mrs. Hue resolutely. "I suppose you've got a point, though. If Charlotte Brandt said you couldn't draw, then it must be true. Of course, she's right about that." She allowed her final words to hang in the air, still looking at Violet and hoping the idea would sink in. There was silence in the little bedroom. Violet opened her mouth to speak, and then closed it.

To heck with dumb old Charlotte "Brat", she thought. *Just because she says something doesn't make it true. Who is she anyway?*

When Violet smiled, her mother knew she'd understood. They exchanged a knowing glance, and a slow smile crept up into one corner of Violet's mouth. Mrs. Hue said, "Violet, I know what Charlotte said hurt your feelings," she said, wiping Violet's cheek. "Remember, though, that you are the only person who can decide what is true for you." Mrs. Hue stood, kissed her daughter's face. "I'm going to start dinner. Come down when you're ready."

Violet nodded and sniffed again. She knew she had some thinking to do. She knew she had to be ready to walk into school tomorrow and deal with Charlotte again. How was she going to do that?

Chapter 4

At recess the following day, Violet, and Amber sat under the big tree watching the other kids play. Violet left her sketchpad at home.

Someone was walking toward them.

"Oh no," said Violet. "Please tell me she's looking for Scarlet or someone."

"Looks like she's headed toward us," said Amber.

Violet rolled her eyes. Her stomach lurched.

"Maybe she's going to apologize for what she said yesterday," Amber guessed. Charlotte stood over the two girls, her hands on her hips, smiling.

"Hi, Violet. Draw any ugly pictures lately?"

"Go away, Charlotte," said Violet. She stood to face her, appearing just a bit taller than she. "Leave me alone," she demanded, finding some courage. But Charlotte was incorrigible.

"Aawwww, what's the matter, Violet? Upset 'cause you can't draw?" She mocked her.

Violet felt her face redden.

"Why are you doing this, Charlotte?"

"Doing what?" Charlotte said, with feigned innocence.

"Teasing me."

"I'm not teasing you. I'm just telling the truth." Then she snapped, "You think you're so hot with your drawing!" Charlotte's face reddened. Why was she getting angry? *She* started this!

"No I don't," said Violet. "What's your problem, Charlotte?"

Before they could argue further, Mr. Cerulean, the playground monitor, intervened.

"Mr. Cerulean, Violet said I have problems!" cried Charlotte.

"I did not!" yelled a shocked Violet.

"Did too!"

"No I…"

"Alright!" exclaimed Mr. Cerulean. "Enough already! Charlotte did you come over here to start trouble with these girls?"

"No," whined Charlotte. "Bu—"

"Go find your friends and leave Violet alone."

"Bu-"

"Go, Charlotte, and leave Violet alone." Mr. Cerulean's voice was firm. Charlotte wouldn't argue. Instead, she pouted and stomped her feet as she walked away.

"Mr. Cerulean, *she* came over here!" explained Violet defensively.

"I know, Violet, I saw what happened. Don't be too hard on Charlotte. You two are very different people."

"Yeah, she's a brat!" spat Violet.

"No," said Mr. Cerulean gently, "There's no need for name calling. Don't get caught up in all that."

" But Mr. C., she keeps bothering me! I don't know what I did to her, but yesterday she came over when I was drawing and insulted my sketch. She said I can't draw and embarrassed me in front of everyone for no reason. I never bothered her."

"I see." said Mr. Cerulean.

"It was like she just came over to cause trouble."

"Violet, everyone knows you like to draw. You're a good artist. Perhaps you could understand that Charlotte might not be so confident." He paused, watching her. "If this happens again, try to walk away from her rather than argue. I'll be around if you need help, though."

Just then the eruption of loud voices caught their attention. Mr. Cerulean left them to go mediate another quarrel among a group of girls. One of them was Charlotte.

Chapter 5

The next day was Friday and Violet was a little apprehensive. She walked into the classroom and looked around. Charlotte wasn't there. She settled into her seat. Mr. Brown, the classroom teacher, announced, "It's almost time for art, boys and girls. Copy your homework before you line up, please."

YES! It was Friday and that meant art class. Violet enjoyed beginning her Fridays with art. It inspired her to draw and practice over the weekends. As the class lined up, she wondered about today's art lesson.

"The different parts of your face are called 'features,'" began Mrs. White. "Can you name some of your facial features?"

Violet knew these, but waited for someone else to answer first.

One girl in the back answered, "Eyes."

"That's right. What other features can you name?"
Violet raised her hand.

"Yes, Violet?" asked Mrs. White.

"Nose and mouth."

"Very good."

The discussion continued: the shape of the head, the ears, which type of line is best for drawing the hair, and so on. "Children, find a partner to work with," instructed Mrs. White. "One person will model while the other person draws their portrait. Afterward, you'll switch roles. That way everyone gets a chance to draw."

The fifth graders walked around the art room connecting with partners. Violet got up from her seat to ask a girl named Emerald to be her partner, when she noticed Mrs. White talking to someone in the front of the classroom. When they parted, Violet's stomach sank like a rock. Charlotte Brandt walked to her table and sat down. She had come to school late. *Great!* Violet thought. *There goes my fine Friday.*

Worse, when Violet turned to go find Emerald, she was walking with Tamlyn James toward two stools in the back of the room. Violet scanned the art room and realized the only person without a partner was Charlotte. *Great,* Violet thought. Charlotte was the last person she wanted to look at right now, much less draw her ugly portrait. She was just about to approach Mrs. White and ask if she could work independently when she felt a tap on her shoulder. Violet turned around to find Charlotte standing in front of her. For a moment they just looked at each other. Then Charlotte said, "Want to be partners?" she asked, smiling at Violet.

"No", Violet replied, and went to find Mrs. White.

Violet explained to Mrs. White the incident on the playground and how she really did not want to work with Charlotte. "She bothers me," Violet explained. "She says mean things, and…" Mrs. White listened, then paused to think. She knew how Charlotte could behave toward some of the other kids. Perhaps this was an opportunity to try something unlikely and see what happened. Mrs. White spoke to both children.

"Well, everyone else is partnered and working already. It's a good thing you got here when you did, Charlotte. You and Violet can help each other."

Suddenly, Charlotte didn't look so thrilled. She had gotten quiet. Well good, Violet wasn't too happy with this arrangement either. Charlotte hadn't said anything to anybody since she walked into the art room. Violet wondered if Charlotte had always looked like this in art, that she simply hadn't noticed. *Well*, she thought, *she's quiet anyway, so what harm would it do to be her partner as long as she stayed that way*?

"Oh, all right," said Violet. She was disappointed but what could she do?

"I want to draw first," Charlotte said hastily.

"Fine," agreed Violet.

She was not about to reveal another drawing to Charlotte so she could make her feel badly about it. Hopefully, class would be over before it was her turn.

Sitting face-to-face, Violet remained still as Charlotte began to draw her portrait. She had missed the discussion on facial features, though, and when Violet tried to help Charlotte said, testily, "I can do it!"

As the endless minutes passed, Violet saw that she could not do it. Charlotte was really having difficulty with the portrait. She had forgotten to draw the guidelines to show where the features went, she drew too small, pressed too hard and got frustrated when she erased.

"Now who can't draw?"

Charlotte's head snapped up. "What?"

There stood Amber, glaring harshly at Charlotte.

"Go away, Amber!" she snapped.

"No. At least Violet can draw a picture. You're picture's ugly."

"Mrs. White!" cried Charlotte. "Amber said my picture is ugly!"

"Amber? That's not like you," said Mrs. White. "What's this all about?"

"I'm just giving Charlotte some of her own medicine. She's been teasing Violet about her drawing and…"

"No, I haven't, I just…"

'Yes, you have, Charlotte Brandt! Don't even lie about it!"

"I'm not lying!"

"Alright, children, alright. Now, that's enough," said Mrs. White.

Violet had sat silently throughout the exchange. This was unbelievable. Everyone was looking at her *again*. She started to speak up, but was promptly shushed by Mrs. White.

Class had practically stopped. The other children stared in anticipation, waiting for whatever would happen next.

Chapter 6

They never got to switch roles, or even finish the portrait. Charlotte and Violet were asked to step outside the classroom with Mrs. White, who realized her idea to pair the two girls had backfired.

"What is going on?" She inquired.

When both girls spoke simultaneously, Mrs. White held up both hands, quieting them. "Aren't you girls friends?"

"Not really," answered Violet. "She keeps bothering me."

"No, I…" Charlotte's voice trailed off as their teacher raised her hand.

"One at a time, Charlotte. Continue, Violet."

"I don't bother her; she keeps getting into my business and into my face and telling me I can't draw and… and…she's just, mean to me." Violet's sensitivities took over as her voice was transformed to a whisper and her eyes welled with tears.

"Okay," said Mrs. White, looking from one girl to the other. "This is bigger than I thought. I'd like the two of you to stay with me when class ends."

As Violet walked home, all she could think about was crossing Miller's field before bumping into Charlotte.

Just get home, she thought. *I don't want to face her, don't want to talk to her. Just get home.*

"AAHHH!" Violet jolted back to reality when her shirt was grabbed from behind. She spun around to find Charlotte, looking very angry.

"You're a tattletale," Charlotte accused.

"I just told Mrs. White what happened, that's all," said Violet. Not wanting to incite Charlotte's anger further, she turned, continuing her walk toward the field.

"Alright, then you're a bi…" Charlotte stopped as two of their classmates approached, also on their way home from school. They wore the same hairstyle, a tightly pulled ponytail, and looked like twins with their matching purses.

"Hey."

"Hey."

"What's going on?"

"I was just about to beat up Violet," said Charlotte.

Violet's heart raced and her wide eyes blinked. *What?* She looked toward the field, wondering how long it would take to run across. She looked at Lavender and Scarlet, the two girls who had just arrived, hoping to garner some sympathy or help. Then she looked at Charlotte, whose eyes met Violet's in a hard stare. They remained that way for what seemed like hours.

Maybe I can talk my way out of it, Violet thought to herself.

" Listen, Charlotte, I don't want to fight."

" Who said anything about fighting? I'm just going to kick your butt all over this field."

The other girls stifled their snickering laughter. When their hands covered their mouths, Violet understood she was alone. They'd be no help to her.

"What did I ever do to you, Charlotte? Why don't you like me?"

"You're a teacher's pet, you had to go and tell."

"Yeah, teacher's pet!" One of the girls colluded.

"You don't even know what happened," Violet shot back.

"So?"

"Go ahead, Charlotte. She'll never tell on you again! Push her down!"

"You do and you'll be sorry."

They all turned to see Amber, standing with both hands on her hips. She stared Charlotte down hard.

"C' Mere Charlotte."

Charlotte remained rooted were she stood. She looked at the two girls by her side.

"Did you hear me? I said come here. Violet might not fight you, but I will." The two latecomers to the tiff quickly quieted. "You afraid?"

"No." Charlotte looked at the two colluders by her side. Nothing.

"Then what's the problem?" Amber stepped forward. "Look, leave Violet alone. She hasn't done anything to you, so stop bothering her."

"Or what?" said Charlotte, suddenly emboldened.

"Or like I said, you'll be sorry," replied Amber, taking another step in Charlotte's direction. Charlotte faltered, stepping back.

The tension was suddenly slackened by what appeared to be a big swirling ball of dust heading toward the girls. Emerging from the center of the dust ball was Mr. Greene's old, dented pick-up truck. He'd pulled up along side the group and stopped.

"Hi, Mr. Greene," smiled Charlotte.

Mr. Greene said nothing, just gawked at the gaggle of girls for a long moment. His squinty eyes and sharp nose resembled the shriveled up visage of a Jack-O-Lantern a month after Halloween. His wrinkled, leathery, pockmarked skin added to the effect.

"You girls okay?" he asked.

"No."

"Yes."

The simultaneous answer from Amber and Charlotte raised Mr. Greene's eyebrows. Violet was amazed to see that he actually had brown eyes under those two big bushy caterpillars above them.

"You sure?"

"Yes," answered Charlotte.

Amber caught Violet's eye, and motioned toward the field with a neat little jerk of her head. Violet nodded her comprehension. As Charlotte smiled, batted her eyes and made up sugary stories to Mr. Greene, Amber and Violet slowly, silently inched aside.

The two other girls stood near the truck, clueless and helpless, not really sure what they were a part of, but wanting to belong anyway.

The sputter of the truck as it pulled away created the perfect diversion for Violet and Amber, who'd grabbed each other's hands and raced across the field together. The swirl of dust left in the truck's wake hid them long enough to gain yards away from their pursuers. Charlotte couldn't catch them. Violet vaguely heard shouting behind them. Something about showing up at school Monday morning.

Chapter 7

"I don't feel good."

"What's the matter?"

"My stomach hurts," said Violet, rolling over in her bed.

"Mmm…" Her mother looked down at Violet, nodding slowly. "Does this have anything to do with school on Friday?"

"No-oooh," Violet moaned. "I feel like I'm gonna throw up." She moaned again, doubling up her body.

"Is everything okay with Charlotte?"

"Fine." Violet avoided her mother's eyes.

"Just fine?"

"Mm-hmm," Violet mumbled from under her covers.

"I see." Mrs. Hue paused. "Anything you'd like to talk about?" she asked.

"No, Mom," Violet whined. "I just don't feel good. I'll go to school tomorrow."

"You're going to feel better tomorrow?" Mrs. Hue asked.

Violet heard the surprise in her mother's voice and scrunched up her face at her mistake. She moaned again, hoping it would sound convincing.

"That sounds bad," said her mother, with furrowed brows. "Alright, then, stay in bed and rest. I'll bring you up some ginger ale."

"Thanks, Mom," Violet said. She exhaled her relief and rolled back over to face the wall.

Violet was sipping her ginger ale when her mother came upstairs an hour later. "Let's get ready then, Violet. Here are your sneakers."

Violet's eyes flew open. "For what?" she asked.

"To go to the doctor," Mrs. Hue replied. "You may have a stomach flu and it's best to help it before it becomes bad." Mrs. Hue gathered up a few stray socks lying on the floor as she spoke, throwing them in the hamper.

Great, thought Violet. She really didn't want to explain to her mother that Charlotte threatened to beat her up on Friday. *Oh, this is so stupid! If I say I feel better, then I have to go to school. If I tell her about Charlotte, she could be mad I didn't tell her, or worse, call Charlotte's mother, or the school.* Violet was at odds with herself. It's not that she thought her mother wouldn't understand. She always handled problems fairly. Should she tell? Violet watched her mother, straightening up her things.

She threw her blanket back, swung her legs over the side of her bed and stepped into her slippers.

"Alright, spill it. What's going on?" Mrs. Hue's voice was gentle, but firm. She patiently waited for an answer during the car ride home from Doctor Verde's office.

"It's nothing, Mom, really."

"It's nothing that's giving you a stomach ache? Look Violet, You've been acting strangely all weekend. The weather's beautiful, yet you haven't left the house. "That's not like you." She paused. "Have you been working on some new drawings?"

"No," said Violet quietly. When she didn't offer more, her mother continued.

"Doctor Verde says there's nothing wrong with you."

"It's alright, I feel better now."

Mrs. Hue looked over at her daughter, who stared straight ahead as they drove home. They remained quiet for the rest of the ride.

Tuesday morning, Violet got dressed, ate breakfast and met up with Amber for the walk to school.

"Where were you yesterday?" Amber asked.

"Didn't feel good," Violet answered briefly. "How was it?" She glanced at Amber to see if her expression belied anything terrible or exciting. "Okay," Amber shrugged. Violet silently hoped today would be quiet, too. They walked the hallway toward Mr. Brown's room.

"Did you tell your parents about Friday with Charlotte?" Asked Amber.

"No," replied Violet. "But my mom knows something's up."

"Gonna tell her?"

"She said she'd be around whenever I decided to talk about what was really going on."

"So she knows you were faking yesterday?" Amber said. "And you didn't get in trouble? Even after going all the way to the doctor?" Amber looked incredulous. "Your mom is so cool. I would have caught it, but good, if I wasted a day like that. *And* made my mom drive and pay for the doctor."

Violet didn't think she'd wasted the day, exactly. "Anyway," she began, but didn't get to finish. The hard tug on her shirt wheeled her backward. The two girls stumbled around the corner, and Amber pushed first into the nearby girl's bathroom.

"What?" Violet asked. Amber faced Violet with her finger over her lips, then turned to peek out the bathroom door. She cased the hallway.

"Lavendar and Scarlet were headed in our direction. I didn't think you'd want to meet up with them," she whispered over her shoulder.

"That's for sure," breathed Violet. "Are they gone?"

Amber peered out into the hall, which emptied as students filed into their classrooms. "Looks clear, let's go," she said.

"Where you going, Scaredy-Cat?" The booming voice echoed off the walls, startling them both. Amber and Violet jolted around to see who the voice belonged to. Suddenly, Violet really was sick to her stomach. "Who are you hiding from?" Charlotte said, standing half out of the last stall. Her hand held the door open while she leaned back, a smug expression on her face, looking as though she had all the time in the world to hang out in the bathroom. As she stepped forward, she said, "Why were you absent yesterday?"

"None of your business," Violet said. "Come on, Amber." Violet reached for the door.

Charlotte pushed it shut, trapping them all in the girl's room. "You tricked me Friday," she said. "You ran away when Mr. Greene drove up. You think I didn't see you, Scaredy-Cat?"

"Don't call me—"

"Scaredy-Cat, Scaredy-Cat," Charlotte taunted.

"I wasn't going to fight you, Charlotte," Violet said. She stood up a little straighter.

"No, you'd rather run away."

"Leave her alone," said Amber.

"Make me," said Charlotte.

Before another word could be said, the door to the girl's room opened and Mrs. Ivory's plump face jutted through. "Why aren't you girls in class?" Her bright green eyes looked to each of them.

"I was just going, Mrs. Ivory, but Violet stood all in my way. I told her I was going to class like I was supposed to and…"

Mrs. Ivory gestured for them to leave and held the door all the way open as the three filed out of the bathroom and headed for class. Violet looked at the floor on the way out, noting the reflection of her unhappy face in shiny hall floor. As they approached their classroom, Mr. Brown stood at the door waiting for them. He looked at each girl as they walked in.

The only one who smiled and said good morning was Charlotte.

As the class bounded on the playground after lunch, Amber went to swing on the swings at the other end of the playground. Violet brought her book to read under the big tree. She was relieved to be out of class with the opportunity to finally be alone.

"Hey, Scaredy—where'd you get those pants? Getting ready for a flood?" Charlotte laughed at her own overused joke. She'd come out the door right behind Violet, who didn't see her in the herd of other kids filing out.

"They're called Capri's," Violet retorted.

"You gonna run through the brook on the way home today, with those floodies?"

Violet walked faster, refusing to answer, or play this stupid game. Her mother had given her these Capri's for her birthday and she thought she looked good in them. She kept walking, trying to increase the distance between herself and Charlotte, who didn't like to be ignored, and so bellowed, "Violet wears floodies!" as she caught up with a few other girls.

Violet caught sight of the small crowd looking at her, and tears welled up in her eyes. They were laughing among themselves and pointing at her pants.

Chapter 8

"Violet!"

She turned to see Charlotte walking toward her. Violet waited.

"Listen, Violet, I'm sorry for what I said about your floo- your pants. My mom said I should try to be a better friend to people. Amanda's mother called and I…well, I sort of got in trouble."

"Oh," said Violet quietly. She hesitated. "You know you really hurt my feelings."

"I'm sorry, Violet. I didn't mean to, I just, I don't know what came over me. You know, I guess I'm just jealous of you. You're so good at art, you're smart and everything."

"You're smart," said Violet.

"You think so?" asked Charlotte.

"Sure," said Violet, smiling. An awkward silence fell between them. Violet shifted from her right foot to her left. She looked at Charlotte. "Do you want…I mean, could we…?"

"Be friends?" Charlotte finished, smiling.

"Yeah," Violet breathed. She couldn't get the words out, thinking it was too much to ask, too good to be true. But Charlotte had understood.

"Of course we can," said Charlotte. "Best friends. Forever."

Violet reached forward to hug Charlotte. Charlotte's face cracked a smile. And didn't stop. Beginning at the corners of her mouth, her face split open in a crooked line, peeling and dividing the skin, revealing a skull covered with slimy, red, steaming goo. Her face slid off and fell to the ground with a disgusting *Plop!* Charlotte's big black bug eyes bulged from their sockets and her long, green forked tongue slithered out from between two rows of sharp, pointy teeth. Charlotte began to laugh a loud, echoing laugh, throwing her head back as she cackled, her jaw shifting unevenly from side to side. Matted clumps of hair from the red gooey head shook in response, dripping small drops of goop to the floor.

Violet recoiled and screamed.

She was still screaming and shaking when her parents came foggily into view. She looked into her mother's eyes and for a moment became silent. Violet slammed her face into her pillow and cried as hard as she ever had in her life. Mrs. Hue rubbed her back to calm her.

"Violet, Honey, why didn't you tell us this was happening?" asked her father.

"I don't know," she said. They sat around the kitchen table together. Mrs. Hue had warmed some milk for them.

"Oh come on, now, Dear. Did you think we wouldn't understand?" he asked. "You know, I have a mind to call Charlotte's mother tomorrow, first thing in the morning, and tell her about her daughter's behavior. She's a bully!"

"Dad, no. Don't call Charlotte's mom," Violet pleaded. "I don't want it to get worse. I'll be okay. I'll just keep to myself, that's all. It'll be alright."

"You tried that," her mother said, bluntly. "She followed you." Violet sipped her milk and stared blankly across the table at nothing in particular. Her mother was right. She could feel her parents' eyes on her face, waiting for her to say something. She felt awkward, yet strangely relieved. She wasn't in trouble. She also wasn't dealing with this by her self anymore. Someone else knew. In the space between a nightmare and a glass of warm milk something had changed. The uncertainty must have played its hand on her face, for her father snapped his fingers in front of her to wake her up. "Violet, are you with us?" he asked.

She looked at him, then her mother. She was exasperated. "I just don't know what to do. I told Charlotte I wouldn't fight her, I try to stay away from her, and I've gone to teachers and told them. Nothing seems to work for me," she finally squeaked. A pang of self-pity twinged inside Violet's chest and she began to cry. "I just want to be friends. I don't do anything to bother her. Why does she bother me? Why does she say mean things to me?" Her mother reached across to touch her hand. "It just hurts my feelings when she makes fun of me," she sobbed, tears running in rivulets down her cheeks. "I'm not a bad person," she sniffed, wiped at her nose and sat up in her chair. Mr. Hue handed her a Kleenex.

"Violet you've done all the right things. Your teachers are looking out for you. They don't always see what you go through, but they care."

"Then why is this so bad?" Violet squeaked.

"Because Charlotte is smart, Violet. Have you ever noticed the times and places where she bothers you?"

"What do you mean?" Mr. Hue was nodding his head emphatically. Whatever her mother was getting at, he agreed with it. She cast her eyes back to her mother, waiting.

"On the playground, in the bathroom, near Miller's field. What's the common denominator?" Violet stared, trying to see where her mother was going. She was about to say she still didn't get when it popped into her head. Just like that. She cocked her head to the side and asked, "Is it that they're all places with only one or two grown ups?" She paused. "Or no grown ups?" She got it. She understood. She wiped her nose. Charlotte would never act up in homeroom; Mr. Brown was always there. In the art room, she was quiet and really didn't start anything. *Oh my gosh*, thought Violet. *Charlotte picks places where she knows she won't get caught bothering people. And if someone does show up, she…."*

"Get it?" Mrs. Hue asked.

"Yes. So, but, how do I handle her?"

"Remember the talk we had in your room? What do you need to remember?"

"That I can decide for myself," she said. She breathed deeply. Saying that sounded so strong, even felt good to her. Even though she knew that dealing with Charlotte might be harder than she thought.

"You know who you are, Violet. Just always remember that. Don't let this situation define you," her mother said. "It's not who you are."

"I'm not a bully," said Violet.

"You are not a victim," confirmed her father.

"I am not a victim," repeated Violet.

Chapter 9

While she no longer brought her sketchpad to school, Violet continued to practice at home. She thought about the school's annual spring art show and thought maybe this year she'd participate. After all, it was her last year in Suregood Elementary. In a few months she would graduate fifth grade and move up to the Middle School.

Violet walked through school with a new sense of strength. She stood a little taller and laughed more with the people who really were her friends.

She had spoken with Mr. Brown and Mrs. White about her problems with Charlotte and felt a little safer. Her teachers were on her side, she knew. She kept clear of Charlotte. Days passed, and Violet's energy was focused on the art show.

One afternoon, after packing up to go home, Violet noticed a piece of paper on her desk. Amber must have left it there. Unfolding the paper, Violet smiled to herself. Amber was her very best friend. She'd kept all their notes to each other since third grade. Notes about homework, boys, after school or weekend plans. When they weren't writing notes they were talking on the phone or at each other's houses or riding bikes or looking at a big, fat elephant with her name written underneath. WHAT?! Turning the drawing over, back to front several times, Violet searched for a name, finding none. This was not from Amber. This wasn't even funny. She looked around the classroom, scanning faces. Amber was involved in a conversation with Emerald. The other kids weren't paying attention to her. They were waiting for dismissal. Violet's eyes settled on Charlotte, writing down homework notes from the board. The corner of her mouth stole upward, as though it were an effort to keep from laughing, as she pretended to concentrate on her note taking.

Dismissal was announced. Children filed out to the buses, the crossing guard and cars driven by parents picking up their kids. Charlotte ran ahead to catch up with Scarlet and Lavendar.

"She kept turning it over to see who it was from," Charlotte laughed. "Duh!" she mocked, crossing her eyes and pulling a face. "You should have seen her face!" The other girls laughed loudly, on purpose, falsely, so that Violet would over hear.

Great, thought Violet. She felt the emotion well up in her chest, daring her to cry. *NO,* she willed herself. *I will not give them the satisfaction of crying. They won't win.* She continued off the school property and caught up with Amber.

"What are you going to do?" Amber asked.

"Nothing."

"Nothing?"

"That's right."

"Isn't that hard? Don't you feel angry?" Amber asked, her voice escalating. "Are you going to tell your Mother?"

"Nope, I'm going to let it go," resolved Violet

"What does that mean?"

"It means I'm not going to get upset over it."

"Can you do that? I couldn't do that, I'd have to go make her eat that piece of paper," said Amber.

"No," said Violet, "that's what she wants. My parents said that if I get upset, she wins. A bully really just wants to make other people upset. Mom said they feel insecure and have no personal power. So, they bother other people."

"What did you do with the note?"

"I crumpled it up and threw it away," answered Violet.

"So what's personal power?"

"It's my own power to decide what's best for me and what is really true for me. You know, what I believe in. I don't believe I look like an elephant, so I threw the paper away. I don't have to play games with Charlotte."

"Didn't it hurt your feelings?"

Violet paused. "When I first saw it and realized it wasn't from you, yeah, I was confused. Then I saw Charlotte at her desk, smiling. Actually, she was trying not to smile, so I figured she wrote it. I got mad. I've been feeling better about things; I wouldn't let myself cry in front of her, so I crumpled the paper up and threw it in the garbage can."

"That was probably a good thing to do in front of her," affirmed Amber. "Now she knows it's not that easy to get to you."

"I guess," said Violet. "I just wish she and the others would leave me alone completely. I see them snickering when I walk by. They look at me and laugh, point at me. I don't know why they like to pick on me," she said. "I do my best to ignore them. I know I am not whatever they think I am, but it's... well, it's still hard to put up with sometimes, even when I walk away."

"Whatever you feel because of them is nothing compared to how insecure they must feel. If all they have to offer is making fun of people and threatening to beat people up, they are going to be very lonely girls. That kind of stuff won't get you friends. Not real friends, anyway." With that, Amber linked arms with Violet.

"You are my very real friend, Violet Hue," said Amber proudly.

"And you are mine," smiled Violet. She swelled up with such a good feeling in her chest, she forgot all about the stupid picture left on her desk. Violet saw that what she had in Amber was real. Really, why should she give Charlotte any more attention? This was who she was: a good friend, a smart girl, a great artist. And yes, at ten years old, she could decide only to be involved with good people. She could respect herself and her own goodness. She knew she would not choose to bully other people after what she'd been through. She'd never make someone feel this bad.

For the next two days, Violet went straight home after school. She was working on some sketches for her art show submission. When she stopped to look at all of her drawings, she frowned. Too many: flowers, faces, animals; she was allowed only one entry in the show. "I have to make a decision," she said aloud to herself. She needed to decide on a subject. But what?

She realized she had mixed feelings about entering work in the show. What if no one liked her art? What if they ridiculed her like Charlotte had on the playground? What if…? *Oh for goodness sake!* She thought to herself. She rolled her eyes at her own negative thoughts. There was just no reason for her to be insecure about this. Violet Hue is a very good artist. Period. Her thoughts drifted back to the art show. *Hmmm…I could enter the flower I sketched, or the portrait project I was working on in art. Or maybe I could do something completely different.*

She decided to stick with the portrait idea. She would talk to Mrs. White after school.

Chapter 10

This year, the Suregood Elementary School art show would be held the third week in April, on the 23rd. Spring had arrived, it stayed light outside much longer; spring smelled fresh and sounded musical, with birds in trees and flying overhead. If you listened carefully, you could even hear the "Quack! Quack!" of the Mallard ducks in the school's courtyard.

Violet knew she had no time to waste in preparing her art for the show, now that she'd decided on her subject. Many Suregood students entered the art show each year. She had spoken to her mother about her own entry and, of course, her mother was thrilled! She hugged Violet tightly. When Violet expressed that she wanted to exhibit her portrait, Mrs. Hue asked to see it. She studied the drawing and after some time, suggested, "How about adding to it, Violet?"

"What do you mean?" asked Violet.

"Well, you've been through a lot recently. I think you're wiser and more confident for how you're handling Charlotte in school. After all, a portrait of a person doesn't only show what they look like, it…"

"…tells about who they are," Violet finished her mother's sentence. She understood what her mother was getting at. Hmmm… something to show who she is. She could use symbolism; make a collage. They talked about symbolism in art and in English when they read stories. Violet's ideas quickly began flowing. She was more determined than ever to be ready by the 23rd.

Chapter 11

By the 21st, Violet's portrait was almost finished. She just had to color the patterns in the background.

She took it downstairs to show her parents.

Mr. and Mrs. Hue looked at the portrait silently. Violet waited. It was building up inside her and she just wanted to tell her parents what the picture was about and what it meant to her.

"Wow, Violet, this is beautiful," her father said. Violet could tell he didn't get it, as usual. So she explained. "It's me- it shows how I like to hide sometimes and do my art alone; that's why the whole right side is blocked out."

"Sounds kind of dark," her father said.

"Dad," Violet said, "It's me. This is the part of me that I don't like to show other people. But the other side shows the entire side of my face, light and colorful.

This part shows the 'me' that has been true to myself. Just like Mom said." Mrs. Hue smiled. "I just have to finish coloring the flowers in the background, then it's finished".

"Why flowers?" asked Mr. Hue.

"'Cause I like flowers," answered Violet.

"Oh," said her father, clearly expecting a more involved answer.

On the 23rd, Violet and her family arrived at the school early in order to walk around the gym and view all the artwork. *Wow!* Violet thought, as she walked around the big boards displaying the pictures. She could see her parents were impressed as well. Her mother, with her hand on her chin, studied some pieces, nodded, and moved on. Mr. Hue seemed to appreciate the pictures, with all their color and childlike skill, though he kept making comments like, "Oh, how pretty," and, "Very nice, very nice." Once, he leaned down and whispered to Violet, "What's this one about?"

Parents and children arrived steadily, milling about the big boards filled with art from students as young as kindergarten right up to fifth grade. The judges walked carefully and thoughtfully around the display boards. Violet watched them write down notes on clipboards as they passed certain works of art. One judge looked at her self-portrait for a long time, but didn't write anything. Then he walked on to the next piece.

People flocked around, eating cookies and drinking juice. Parents were asking, "How's everything?" to each other, talking about their families, how this school year is nearly over and can you believe they're going to middle school next year?

Violet turned her attention to the buzzing sound of the microphone as Mrs. White stepped up to greet the crowd gathered in the gym.

"May I have your attention, please?"

Everyone stopped talking and looked at Mrs. White as she addressed the throng of people before her. "Good evening, everyone and welcome to our annual art show at Suregood Elementary. I hope everyone has had an opportunity to see all the wonderful work our student artists have displayed this evening. At this time, it is my pleasure to announce the names of students who will receive Ribbons of Honor for their work. Names for Honorable Mention will follow." She paused before saying, "The Third Place ribbon goes to…"

The auditorium was silent, every child waiting to hear their name and every parent hoping to hear their child's name.

The list was read slowly:

"Michael Andrews…" Clapping and cheering erupted from the crowd.

Violet clapped for Michael. She looked around, wondering if her name would be called. Glancing at her portrait, Violet questioned whether she had put enough work into it.

"Sienna Mendez…" Sienna's family hugged her tightly, smiling so that Violet thought their faces might freeze that way. Sienna walked up to accept her ribbon. Violet crossed her fingers behind her back.

She looked down at the floor, and realized she was holding her breath.

Violet slowly let out her breath and let her shoulders fall. *I shouldn't expect so much,* she thought to herself. She looked ahead at Mrs. White, who was about to read the next name. There was only one more Ribbon of Honor left to announce. Before the name could be announced, the list fell out of Mrs. White's hand and floated to the floor. She bent down to retrieve it. Violet's hands were still behind her back; her fingers were crossed so tightly the knuckles turned white. She shifted her weight from foot to foot. Mrs. White took a moment to compose herself before announcing the name for First Place ribbon of honor.

Oh, I can't stand it! Violet thought to herself loudly. She looked down at the floor, then up at the ceiling. *Why doesn't she ju…*

"…let Hue…"

Violet snapped to attention. "What? What did she say?"

"Violet, go up and accept your ribbon! You won!" Her parents clapped, hugged Violet, then all but pushed her up toward Mrs. White, who was clapping and smiling. Violet faced the crowd. They were clapping for her. She felt heat rising in her face and ears, even as she smiled and humbly said, "Thank you."

Mrs. White's voice faded as Violet walked back to stand near her portrait, "…for Honorable Mention, the names are…"

Violet had taken first place for her self-portrait, entitled, 'The Light and Dark of Violet Hue'. She did it!

Violet Hue is a successful artist. And apparently, she's not the only one who thinks so.

On Monday, the school was still buzzing about the art show and Violet's self-portrait. Both teachers and students congratulated her.

During a break to the bathroom, Violet found herself heading down the hall toward none other than Charlotte Brandt, who looked around to find her cohorts, but saw no one. Violet said nothing as they passed each other. "Congratulations, Violet," Charlotte said. Then, under her breath, she snorted, "Loser."

"Excuse me?" Violet whirled around. They stood facing each other, staring silently. She had Charlotte's attention.

"What?" shrugged Charlotte.

"I heard what you said," said Violet.

"So? What are you going to do about it?" challenged Charlotte.

Violet said nothing. She froze. What was she going to do about it? They were the only two people in this hallway. Now would really be her chance to give Charlotte some of her own medicine, tell her what a loser *she* was, maybe even push her down to show her who was really stronger. After all, she had threatened to beat Violet up. One good push would show her. Violet looked all around, took a step toward Charlotte, her stare steadfast, then…

Chapter 12

...She stopped. What was she thinking? How could she even think of using her hands on another person? Well, she could think of it, she was that frustrated. She'd had enough of this. It would stop now, but not through pushing or fighting. Her stomach felt a little sick and her hands were shaking. She stood face to face with her bully.

"You know what, Charlotte? You're a bully. And I don't understand why you're picking on me all the time, but I've had enough. I think you're insecure and I feel sorry for you, because the only way you can make friends is to get other insecure people to agree with what you say. You're not a nice person. You're mean. Why would anyone want to *be* friends with you, Charlotte? You treat people like dirt, you're disrespectful and...well, just a mean bully with no real friends. How does that feel? It's the truth. I've been getting upset with the things you've said about me and they're not even *true*! The truth about you is that you'll never have a true friend until you can *act* like one, until you can stop calling people names, stop talking about them and threatening to hurt them. That's the saddest truth of all and I feel sorry for you. Now, I'm telling you," said Violet forcefully, pointing a finger at Charlotte's face, "leave-me-alone!"

Charlotte's face fell. She stood, frozen. Then she spoke so meekly it could hardly be heard.

"We could be friends…"

"No we couldn't," replied Violet. "My friends respect me." Again she pointed her finger in Charlotte's face, looking her square in the eyes, finishing with, "You don't have enough of that to be my friend."

Violet left Charlotte standing in the hall. Alone. Embarrassed. Several kids had piled up around the corner, having seen and heard the altercation. A few of them looked at Charlotte and covered their mouths as they snickered, or just stood looking at her. Then they followed Violet back into the classroom.

Violet was again inspired to bring her sketchpad to school that Tuesday. At recess, under the big tree on the playground, she reached for her pencils and erasers as she had just a few short weeks ago. She took a deep breath and looked around. This time, Violet knew she had nothing to fear, for now she was certain Charlotte Brandt would not be harassing her anymore.

Violet began bringing her sketchpad to school so often that other students began to bring theirs. They shared ideas, pencils and crayons, and many happy hours drawing pictures.

"Let's call ourselves something," suggested Emerald.

The other artists looked at her.

"A name, I mean. Let's give ourselves a name, like our own art club name."

The others thought about it a minute, then Henry came out with, "How about the Suregood Sketch Club?"

"What about the Suregood Sketchers?" asked Amber. Simple. They all agreed. From that day on, they were the Suregood Sketchers. They met every day at recess, art supplies in hand, ready to draw. They bothered no one and accepted anyone, but…no bullies allowed. To join, you had to have an attitude of respect and positivity.

Violet Hue knew now that *courage* wasn't about having no fear; it was doing something even though you were nervous or afraid. That taking a risk could help you grow as a person. Violet had courageously taken her sketchpad to school and dealt with Charlotte Brandt, entered the art show and won! Her own personal power had helped her stand up to Charlotte. Now, she has inspired other kids to pursue their own art. *Look at that,* she reflected.

She remembered her mother's words: "Only you can decide what is true for you, Violet. Follow it, and don't let a bad situation define who you are."

After the Story Activities

Thoughtful Questions and Activities:

1. Create a self-portrait collage, using a variety of materials. How do you see yourself both inside and out?

2. Write a letter to someone whose words have hurt your feelings. Tell them how you feel in the letter (you don't have to show it to them).

3. Make a list of at least 10 great things about YOU! Write a letter to yourself expressing how wonderful you are and how grateful you are to have all the good things you have.

4. Which character in the story do you identify with most? Whom do you wish you could identify with more?

Glossary

1. **mediate**: to help two opposing sides come to an agreement.
2. **symbolism**: the use of symbols or pictures to represent ideas.
3. **forgive**: to stop being angry at the way someone has treated you.
4. **portrait**: a picture of a person, with emphasis on their face.
5. **self-portrait**: a picture of yourself.
6. **courage**: doing something despite being afraid.
7. **collage**: a piece of artwork made with many different materials: paints, newspaper, thread, magazine pictures, and whatever else you can find.
8. **risk**: taking a chance on doing or having something.

10 Ways to Help Your Child Handle Bullies

1. Build your child's self-confidence. Offer praise and point out your child's strengths.
2. Help your child develop verbal defenses against bullies, such as, "Stop, right now!" "I will tell my parents (or teacher)." Role play with your child.
3. Tell your child to look bullies in the eye and speak firmly.
4. Let your child know it's okay to tell on a bully and to ask for help from a trusted adult.
5. Teach your child to avoid body language and words that put them in danger.
6. Encourage healthy friendships so your child learns how to be a good friend and seek out good friends.
7. Instruct your child to always walk and play with a buddy, and to avoid unsafe areas such as dark hallways and alleys.
8. Help your child learn to silently repeat phrases that boost confidence in difficult situations, such as, "I am a strong person."
9. Assure your child that it's okay to walk away from bullies and seek a place of safety.
10. If the problem is serious, ask your child's teacher or principal to confront the bully or the bully's parents if necessary.

Acknowledgements

I'd like to thank a boy who, on an eighth grade field trip, told me in front of the whole class that I could not draw, as I sat with my own pad and pencils. It was the initial inspiration for this story.

To all my kids (past and present) at Valley Cottage, who inspire me, this story is for you. May it serve to remind you of your own personal power and how great you truly are.

I also want to acknowledge my friends and colleagues Helen Davies, who helped as proof-reader and copy editor for this story and my first book, **The Courtyard Duck;** Karen Pesner and Isabel Valenzuela for the photographs; Carolyn Travers, thank you for your time and constructive feedback. Thanks to *all* my colleagues at V.C. for your support and encouragement. You are truly the warmest, most dedicated team in any school anywhere! I am blessed to be among you!

About the Author

Jacqueline Mahan teaches art in Nyack, NY to children in grades kindergarten through five. She also works with adult painters during the spring and fall seasons in her watercolor workshop. Ms. Mahan is a published poet, with work in three anthologies by the International Society of Poets. She is the author of *The Courtyard Duck (2004),* and has served as the illustrator for *Tree of Music, The Mpingo Pingo Tree,* by Oona'o Haynes.

Ms. Mahan holds a degree in fine art from Rockland Community College, a BA in art education from St. Thomas Aquinas College and MA in art education from the College of New Rochelle. She is featured in *Who's Who in American Education* and *Who's Who in America,* by Marquis Publishing.

She currently makes her home in Orange County, NY.

CPSIA information can be obtained at www.ICGtesting.com
Printed in the USA
BVOW021048160712

295315BV00001B/21/A